Published by Hawthorn Press, Hawthorn House, 1 Lansdown Lane, Stroud, Gloucestershire, GL5 1BJ, UK. Tel: (01453) 757040. E-mail: info@hawthornpress.com www.hawthornpress.com

English edition, Pancakes for Findus, © Hawthorn Press 2007
Text and illustrations © Sven Nordqvist
Translation by Julia Marshall and Penelope Todd and edited by Nathan Large
Typeset in Palatino by Winslade Graphics
Printed in Latvia by Livonia Print 2014, 2015, 2017, 2020

British Library Cataloguing in Publication Data applied for

ISBN 978-1-903458-79-2

Pancakes for Findus

Sven Nordqvist

Hawthorn Press

2 There was once a man called Pettson who had a cat named Findus. They lived in a little red house with a tool shed, a hen house, an outside toilet, a woodshed and a garden. Paddocks lay all around, and beyond them was the forest.

The neighbours thought Pettson was odd. He was certainly absentminded. And it wasn't normal, the way he talked to that cat.

But none of this would have mattered, if Gustavsson hadn't told everyone how Pettson made pancakes out of his own trousers. And how he climbed over the roof to get to the shop. And how he had tied a curtain to the cat's tail. Gustavsson had seen it with his very own eyes!

It all happened on Findus' birthday.

Findus had three birthdays a year, because it was more fun that way.
And every birthday, Pettson made him a pile of pancakes.

This birthday Pettson went to the hen house to collect a basket of
eggs. Then he sat on the bench outside the kitchen and polished them.
Pettson was a tidy man and he wanted them all clean and shiny.
Findus paced up and down, keen to get started.

'Do you absolutely have to clean all the eggs?' he asked crossly.

'I'll have another birthday before we get our pancakes.'

'Sooo, you're that impatient,' said Pettson. 'Come on, let's get cooking. Three eggs should do. Now we'll see if we can make some pancakes.'

'Of course we can make pancakes,' said Findus. He was already inside looking for the frying pan.

They left the rest of the eggs outside on the bench.

Pettson cracked the eggs into a bowl.

'Now we need milk and sugar … a little salt, some butter …'

He went to find them in the pantry.

'But where has the flour got to? Have you eaten the flour, Findus?'

'I have certainly not eaten the flour,' said Findus indignantly.

'Must have been me, then' muttered Pettson, scratching his nose.

He looked three times through the pantry, in the wood stove, the wardrobe and the seat, but he couldn't find the flour.

'Bother,' he said. 'I'll have to bike to the shop. Wait here, Findus. I'll be right back.'

But Findus was sick of waiting. He shot out the door before Pettson.

Pettson's bike had a puncture.

'How did that happen? Have you bitten a hole in my tyre, Findus?' he grumbled.

'I certainly do not bite holes in tyres,' said Findus indignantly.

'Must have been me, then' muttered Pettson, pulling his ear.

'Never mind. I'll fix it. Wait here, Findus, while I get the tools from the shed. Then I'll fix the puncture, bike to the shop for some flour, and we can get on with the pancakes.'

But Findus couldn't wait, so he ran on ahead.

But when Pettson went to open the tool shed door, it was locked.

And the key was gone.

'What next?' he said. 'This door's never locked. Have you lost the key, Findus?'

'I certainly never lose keys,' said the cat indignantly.

'Then it must have been me. This is a bother,' muttered the old man, rubbing his eyes. He peered through the window, and tried the door again, but it was still locked.

Then Findus whistled and pointed down the well.

Pettson hurried over.

'My goodness, there's the key! How did it get down there? And how will I get it out?'

Biting on his lip, he pondered a while. And then he got it.

'I know! I can put a hook on a long stick and fish up the key. Do you have a long stick, Findus?'

'I've certainly never had a long stick,' said Findus, not sure whether to be indignant or not.

'Then I must have one somewhere,' said Pettson, scratching his hat.

'Wait here while I go and look. Then I can fish up the key, so we can get into the tool shed, so I can fix the bike, so I can buy the flour, so we can make your pancakes.'

But the cat couldn't wait so he ran on ahead.

Pettson and Findus hunted
high and low for a long
stick. They looked in the hen
house, behind the tool shed,
in the garden, the woodshed,
the pantry and under the
sofa. But they couldn't find
a long stick anywhere. Then
Pettson remembered he had
a fishing rod up in the tool
shed loft.

'The rod will be perfect,' said Pettson.

'But first I need the ladder, to climb the roof to get into the loft.'

'The ladder's behind the woodshed in Anderson's paddock,' he said, 'and Anderson's bull is sleeping on it. He'll go berserk if I move it.'

'We'll have to trick him, Findus. How will we do that?'

Pettson stroked his beard and thought so hard you could almost hear his brain buzzing.

After a long time he asked Findus, 'Are you any good at bullfighting?'
'Nooo, I've never fought a single bull,' said Findus, alarmed.

'That's a shame,' said Pettson. 'Because if we can't move the bull, I can't get the ladder, so I can't get the rod from the loft, so I can't fish the key up from the well, so I can't get into the shed to get the tools to fix the bike, so I can't buy flour and there won't be any pancakes. What sort of a birthday would it be without pancakes?'

Findus sat a moment then he said: 'But I've seen off the odd cow, of course. So I should be able to see off that old bull, at a pinch.'

'You must be feeling hungry for pancakes by now,' said Pettson slyly. 'I'll just go and get what we need. Wait here,' he said. 'Back soon.'

He took down one of the flowery yellow curtains in the kitchen, and fetched the old gramophone and a record from the living room.

Then he went out to Findus. He tied the curtain to his tail.

'They use curtains like this for bull fighting in Spain,' said Pettson. 'Get ready to run — but not till I say so!'

He put the gramophone by the fence where the bull was sleeping. He put the record on and set it going. A man started singing,

'My Bonny lies over the ocean…'

'This'll wake him up,' he chuckled.

'My Bonny lies over the sea!'
The bull woke with a start
and looked wildly about.

The song made him cross, and then
even crosser. He swiped at a passing
bumblebee. That didn't stop the noise.
Then he spun round and saw Pettson
and the cat and the gramophone. That
was it!

He put his head down and pawed
at the ground to get a good take-off.
Then he tensed all his muscles and
thundered straight at them.

'Now!' shouted Pettson.

'Run as fast as you can!'

Findus flew like a comet
with a red and yellow tail.
The bull wheeled about
and chased it. He'd
get that noisy
curtain!

When the bull had gone, Pettson slithered under the fence. He snatched the ladder and sneaked back, just as the cat whizzed by with his flying yellow tail.

Across the paddock, the exhausted bull was puffing hard and wondering what had happened.

Findus couldn't stop. He whizzed past the bench. The curtain caught the basket and tipped the eggs out, splat!

Pettson tripped on the curtain and fell down flat! in the eggy mess. Not one egg was left whole.

Pettson said a lot of words he shouldn't have. He picked himself up from the sticky puddle.

'Why did you put that basket on the bench, Findus? Look at the mess it's made!'

'I certainly never put it there!' hissed the cat indignantly.

'Must have been me, then!' spat Pettson back.

Then, because it was Findus' birthday, he calmed down.

'This is awful,' he sighed. 'I can't stand this mess. I'll have to clean it up before I make the pancakes.'

He took a shovel and started to heave the eggy slop into a bucket.

That's when Gustavsson came nosing along.

'Hello Pettson, busy as usual I see,' he said, trying to work out what was in the bucket.

'Not really. We're celebrating a birthday, so I'm just making a pancake mix,' said Pettson. 'We're making a huge pile of pancakes.' He shovelled the last of the egg mixture into the bucket.

'There,' he said, wiping his hands on his trousers. His trousers were very eggy.

'I could use a new pair, actually. These are over thirty years old,' he thought, and took them off.

'I might as well pop these into the mixture. If you only have a birthday three times a year you should do it properly,' he said and shoved the trousers into the bucket.

Gustavsson gaped at the mess. Pancake batter! He sneaked a look at Pettson. The old man must be crazy! Best pretend nothing was wrong.

'I see, so, pancakes for you and the cat? That sounds good!'

'Absolutely, my own recipe,' said Pettson proudly. 'But first I must go and buy some flour. Wait here; I'll be right back.'

He took the ladder to the tool shed, climbed the roof and disappeared over the top.

Gustavsson stood there, looking at the roof. Then he looked at the muddy egg mixture in the bucket, and at the cat pacing about with a floral curtain tied to his tail. He looked at the old gramophone which was stuck singing: '… bring back my Bon—bring back my Bon—bring back my Bon …' He looked back at the roof, where he last saw Pettson.

'The shop's in the other direction,' he muttered. He went home looking very confused.

Meanwhile, Pettson squeezed into the loft, and eventually found the fishing rod.

He climbed down and tied a hook to the end of the rod. He went to the well and fished up the key.

With the key he opened the door to the tool shed. He got his tools and fixed the puncture. He biked to the shop and bought the flour and a new pair of trousers.

Then he came home and made a huge pile of pancakes for Findus.

They sat in the garden and drank tea and ate pancakes and played waltzes on the gramophone, as they always did when Findus had a birthday.

As far as Findus was concerned, there wasn't anything wrong with Pettson at all.

Pancake Recipe

5 eggs

600 ml/21 fl oz/2.5 cups milk

2 tbsp sugar

1 tsp salt

500 ml/18 fl oz/2 cups self-raising flour

100 ml/4 fl oz/0.5 cups water

2 tbsp butter

200 ml/7 fl oz/0.8 cups double cream

Jam

1. Mix the 5 eggs, half the milk, sugar and salt.

2. Add the flour and mix until smooth with no lumps. Add the remaining milk and water. Leave to sit for a moment.

3. In a frying pan melt the butter and add this to the mix so you don't have to use so much butter between pourings. Cook the pancakes and let them cool.

4. Whip the cream. Spread the cream and jam alternately on the pancakes. Decorate.

ORDERING BOOKS

If you have difficulties ordering Hawthorn Press books from a bookshop,
you can order from our website **www.hawthornpress.com**,
or direct from our UK distributor BookSource,
Tel: 0845 370 0067, Email: **orders@booksource.net**

Findus and Pettson Books from Hawthorn Press

Hawthorn Press